How many angels can dance
on the head of a pin?
        —an old question

BARBARA HELEN BERGER

Angels on a Pin

PHILOMEL BOOKS

What if there was a city on a pin?

What if
it was no bigger than a speck of dust?
But the people who lived there
didn't know that.

To them, it was the biggest, the best,
the only city in the world.

Sometimes that made them feel lonesome.

Then one day, somebody made a discovery.
"Hey wow, look! Another city!"

So they all set off on a grand expedition
to see if anybody was there.

From that other city came whistles and shouts,
"Hey wow, look! We're not alone!"

To celebrate,
the mayor blew his trumpet.
Then the boogie-woogie began.

Bebop-a-loola, sha-na na-na na.

Shimmy shimmy hip hop, and cha-cha-cha.

People heard the hoopla from far, far away.

So they set off on grand expeditions.

From pin to pin and beyond they flew—

like clouds of boogie-woogie dust.

From every city came whistles and shouts,

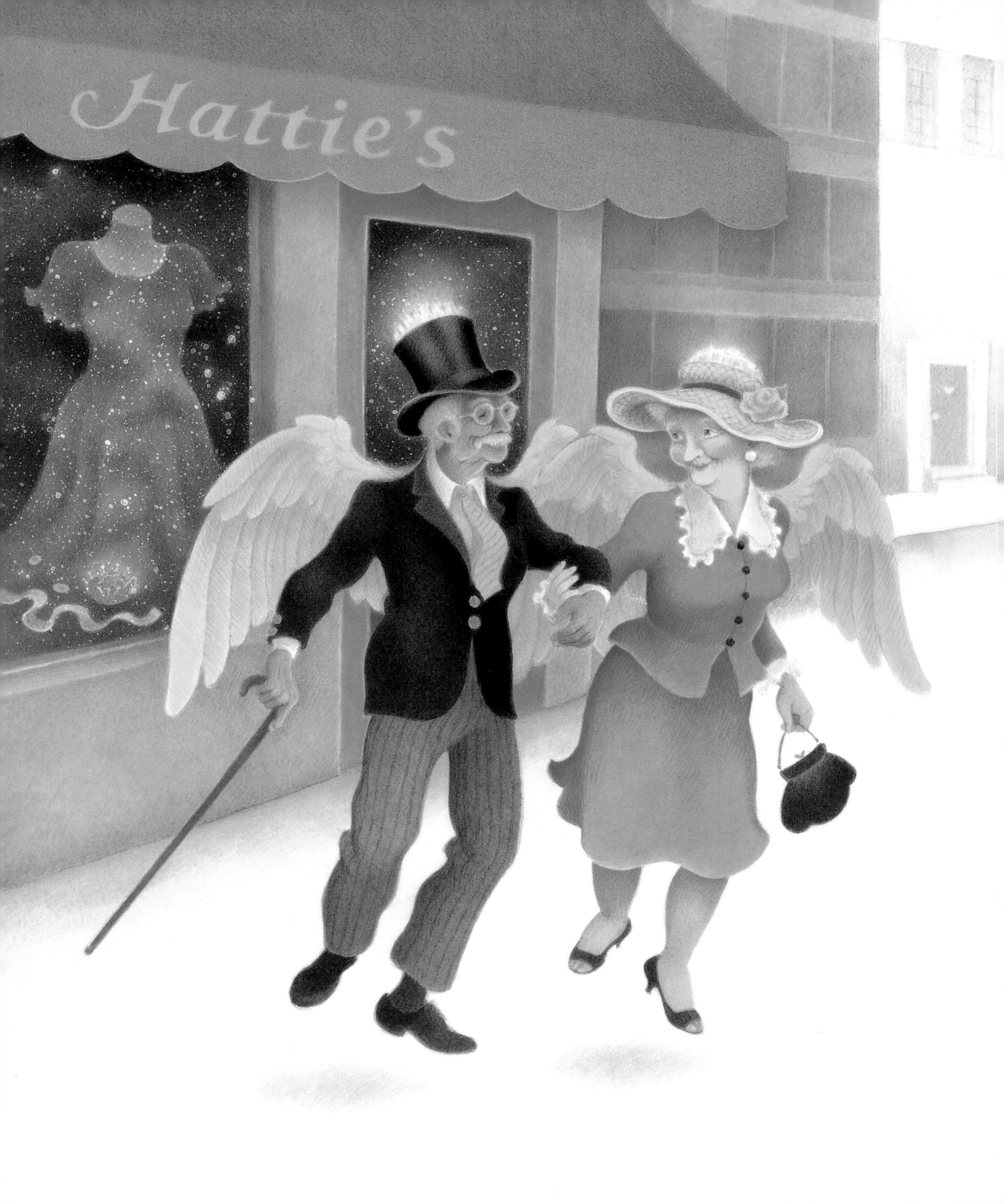
Hattie's

"Hey wow, look! We're not alone!"

To Sorrel and Gus

Patricia Lee Gauch, editor.

Text and illustrations copyright © 2000 by Barbara Helen Berger. All rights reserved. This book, or parts thereof, may not be reproduced in any form without permission in writing from the publisher, Philomel Books, a division of Penguin Putnam Books for Young Readers, 345 Hudson Street, New York, NY 10014. Philomel Books, Reg. U.S. Pat. & Tm. Off. Published simultaneously in Canada. Printed in Hong Kong by South China Printing Co. (1988) Ltd. Book design by Gunta Alexander. The text is set in Administer. The art was done in acrylic, colored pencil, and pastel on hot pressed watercolor paper. Library of Congress Cataloging-in-Publication Data   Berger, Barbara, 1945 Mar. 1– Angels on a pin / Barbara Helen Berger   p.   cm. Summary: The people living in a tiny city on a pin, thinking that theirs is the biggest city in the world but feeling lonesome, discover another city on another pin and rejoice that they are not alone. [1. Cities and towns—Fiction. 2. Size—Fiction.] I. Title. PZ7.B4513An 2000 [E]—dc21 98-6942 CIP AC   ISBN 0-399-23247-8   10 9 8 7 6 5 4 3 2 1   First Impression